BLACK CAT ANTHOLOGY:

*A Collection of all three books
in the Black Cat series.*

BLACK CAT:

Unfulfilled and Unlucky

"People trust me with their mental health; they shouldn't."

BLERB

Blerb:

Jay Swan is a scruffy, weak and melancholic psychiatrist from Columbia. His life is going nowhere until he meets Elizebeth Songbird, a beautiful, enchanting woman with a passion for love.

Jay takes an instant liking to Elizebeth and the thoughtless and brutal ways she did things she learnt during her years in the city.

However, when a traumatic event happens to Jay, Elizebeth springs to the rescue. Jay begins to notice that Elizebeth is actually rather happy at heart.

But, the pressures of Elizebeth's job as a gardener leave her blind to Jay's affections and Jay takes up adventures to try and distract himself from his seemingly one sided crush.

Finally, when Elizebeth had enough she decided to act as Jay had done so long ago.. But will she ever find the everlasting love that she wants or deserves?

CHARACTER BIOS

Character Bios:

Jay Swan A 32-year-old Psychiatrist is traumatised by the loss of his left arm when he was Fourteen. Physically, he is built a bit like a scruffy blob. His top quality is that he is particularly straightforward and emotionally numb. He is striving to find acceptance of happiness and the regrets of his love life.

Elizabeth Songbird is A 31-year-old brash woman from the city who can only smile by day while working as a gardener. Physically, she is built like an elegant beautiful cat. She strongly dislikes her job and has been searching for her long lost friend and love interest.

LIFE BEFORE COLUMBIA

Life Before Columbia:

Jay Swan grew up with his childhood friend Elizebeth Songbird and despite his traumatic loss of his arm they stuck together in the city. Jay eventually ends up with a job as a Psychiatrist and Elizebeth as a gardener both riding the waves of life that came their way.

THE MOVE

The Move:

A few years later on Jay's 22nd Birthday he made a wish to explore the world a bit and move away from the city, knowing his Job was safe with remote screening now being implemented for all those who were relying on his health advice, he made up his mind and with a heavy heart he told Elizebeth of his plans.

Elizabeth, shocked and jealous, was not happy with Jay's plan to move; she thought they would stick together as they had always done, but not wanting to trample his dreams she stayed silent and supportive of his ideas hiding the fact she was hating her job as a gardener and only enjoyed life because of Jay's presence in it.

LIFE IN THE CITY

Life In The City:

After he departed Elizebeth came to regret not telling him one last thing she had been wanting to tell him all along, her feelings toward him and how she wanted to spend her life with him. Little did she know that in a cruel twist of fate he had the same feelings but never shared them as she had also done.

A few months later Elizebeth stopped...

THE SEARCH

The Search:

She no longer wanted to just toil away at a job she hated, regretting things not said and actions not undertaken. She, much like Jay, made a decision. A decision to find her friend, her love interest after all this time.

Unfortunately she never knew where exactly Jay had gone but nonetheless she searched and it wasn't until a few years later she had finally done it. She had found the address.

Columbia...

LIFE IN COLUMBIA

Life In Columbia:

Jay, unaware of Elizabeth's feelings and search, was living his everyday life, working and relaxing at home. He, much like many others, took up drinking as a bit of mental numbing whenever his traumatic thoughts came circling back and this was his life for the years between the city and Columbia.

REUNITED

Reunited:

On a day much like any other, Jay Swan finished his work and returned home for a well deserved drink as he did day to day for years since moving to Columbia, but today was a little different he was thinking about Elizebeth Songbird again. Elizebeth was the beautiful melancholic childhood fiend he once had with enchanting eyes and soft skin and for the longest time secret crush before the move out of the city.

Jay walked over to the window holding his drink and reflected on his happy surroundings. He had always hated this "Heavenly" Columbia with its curved, clear cloud and fresh air. It was a place that encouraged his tendency to feel Happy… an emotion he very much hated after leaving his friend behind in the city, an emotion he felt he no longer deserved. Trying to numb this feeling he continues his drink.

Then whilst looking through the window he saw something in the distance, or rather some*one*. Could it be? The beautiful figure of Elizebeth Songbird?

Jay rubbed his eyes thinking he was seeing things after only a sip of his drink but as he kept looking it became more and more apparent she was real and she was headed toward him.

Jay gulped. He rushed to the mirror and glanced at his own reflection. "Do I look okay?" he thought. He started telling himself repeatedly that he was a strong, disenchanted whiskey drinker; everything will be fine, nothing to worry about, right?. He then remembered something that he didn't want to recall, the memories of his family and how they viewed him, how they saw him as a lazy, jittery liar with nothing to do but drink all the livelong day and complain. "Is this how she's going to view me now too?" He thought.

After this he proceeded to pour away his drink and hide the bottles that were lying about the room, he didn't want to give off the wrong impression after so long apart, he glanced out the window again to see how much time he had before she arrived.

Trying to psych himself up for Elizabeth's arrival he recounted an event that made him feel strong and useful, the time he had even helped a cruel heathen recover from a driving accident even if they were undeserving of the help.

But not even this "strong" person he tried to remember and embody, the one who had once helped a cruel Heathen, was prepared for what Elizebeth had in store for him today.

The rain started hammering like racing dogs at a track, causing Jay to become increasingly depressed and worried. Jay, trying to calm himself, grabbed a smooth stone that had been strewn nearby; and started to massage it with his fingers.

As Jay stepped outside and Elizebeth came closer, he could see the colossal smile on her face and started to think that everything might just be alright even if it's raining and completely unexpected. He was going to see his friend again; he was finally going to be able to speak with her and tell stories of his time in Columbia.

This however was not going to be the case…

As Elizebeth arrived she gazed at him with what seemed to be the affection of over 9000 wise Lovebirds. Suddenly out of nowhere she said, in somewhat hushed tones, "I love you and I want your ever loving embrace.".

Jay looked back at her, even more confused, twisted up and depressed than before still massaging his smooth stone. "Elizebeth, I … I…," he replied, unable to respond to her confession, his mind racing with responses and outcomes of answers he thought to say.

Time seemed to crawl by as they looked at each other with sad confused feelings, like two hungry cats starving at a very emotionless shelter, a shelter that he imagined had slow piano music playing in the background and two old people contemplating its everlasting sombre sad beat.

Jay looked back and studied Elizebeth's soft skin and enchanting eyes, thinking as he did of what to say to her.Thinking of that thought made aloud. Eventually, he took a deep breath. "I'm sorry," began Jay in apologetic tones, "but I no longer feel the same way, and I think I never will. I just don't love you anymore Elizebeth. It's been too long."

Elizebeth looked completely devastated, her emotions visible and raw like a wild, hunting lion. Her years of searching for nothing, her anguish and regret visible for all to see.

Jay with his eyes closed and head in his hands could actually hear Elizebeth's emotions shatter into a thousand tiny pieces. When he glimpsed up at the sound he thought he had heard, he saw the beautiful melancholic Elizebeth with tears in her eyes hurry away into the distance never to be seen again.

Jay slowly returned to his room, closing the window and blocking out the sound of the rain and thought to himself about everything that had just suddenly unfolded before him, after a while thoughts came flooding to mind

"Not even a glass of Whiskey would calm my nerves tonight, not now".

"I'm an idiot!"

"Why did I say that?"

"I do love her, I do, Why did I say that?"

"I'll never see her again"

Jay began to spiral in his thoughts sinking deeper and deeper into his own despair.

A few days later It was a sleepy day accentuated by the ruddy sleet.

It was hard to believe that in a few moments, I would suffer a sudden sensational death.

I was thinking deftly as I trembled with gleeful joy, like a beautiful flower loving the sunlight in the summer. As I strolled down some back alleys in the wrong area of Columbia searching for problems and a way to die.

The thoughts of Elizebeth and that day are still repeating in my head over and over.

The culprit of my death, a cat , had a sleepy face and dull claws. It didn't look dangerous. Not even its black fur and scars warned me of my fate.

I should have sensed the danger in its staring evil eyes. It's ominous nature and the aura it gave off but I didn't.

Even when searching for a way to die I thought I would be the one to control how it happened but nothing could have prepared me for how I ended up.

A cat... that's really how I went... A cat...

All I can still vividly recall is the blood coming down onto my hands from my neck like a red waterfall and one singular sound - *Hisss*. And then... Darkness...

My life slipped away.

I hope if anyone, only dearest Elizebeth weeps for me.

THE END OF BOOK 1

BLACK CAT DEUX:

Love and Lucky

"I only ever met one women I'd ever call truly caring."

BIOS

Bios:

Jay Swan A 32-year-old Psychiatrist is traumatised by the loss of his left arm when he was Fourteen. Physically, he is built a bit like a scruffy blob. His top quality is that he is particularly straightforward and emotionally numb. He is striving to find acceptance of happiness and the regrets of his love life.

Elizabeth Songbird is A 31-year-old brash woman from the city who can only smile by day while working as a gardener. Physically, she is built like an elegant beautiful cat. She strongly dislikes her job and has been searching for her long lost friend and love interest.

"I only ever met one woman I'd call truly caring."

RECAP

Recap:

Jay and Elizebeth both grew up in the city, Jay moved to Columbia, Elizabeth stayed in the city, Elizabeth quits job, Starts searching for Jay, Arrives to find out no love, Elizabeth leaves, Jay is attacked by a cat.

DETERMINATION

Determination:

Jay with his eyes closed and head in his hands could actually hear Elizebeth's emotions shatter into a thousand tiny pieces. When he glimpsed up at the sound he thought he had heard, he saw the beautiful melancholic Elizabeth with tears in her eyes hurrying away into the distance never to be seen again…

Or so he thought, Elizabeth after learning of Jay's feelings towards her or lack thereof did take off into the distance but not to leave forever as Jay assumed, she left to collect her thoughts and to formulate a plan to get Jay to love her back after all this time.

Thoughts of the storied past they spent together crossed her mind and in that moment she remembered little things Jay liked to do and as such she began her plan to bring about the "magic" of love between them.

After a few days of planning and thinking, thinking and planning Elizebeth was finally ready to return to Jay, ready to change his mind, ready to fight for what she wanted in life. This new found determination would lead her back to Jay's house to once again speak with him.

WHERE'D HE GO?

Where'd he go?

On a sleepy day accentuated by ruddy sleet, Elizebeth set off once again to Jay's house ready and raring to go, ready to fight for Jay.

Elizabeth was getting closer to Jay's house now after a slow trudge through the wet sleet and rain she eventually saw the house came into view. Elizabeth noticed the windows closed and completely covered with no light entering the house or leaving the house. Now this was odd she thought, sure it's cold but it's day time, it's light out, why would the windows be covered? A shiver went down her spine and she started to think something isn't right, as these thoughts came to mind she started rushing to the door of Jay's house uneasy of this feeling she now has.

AN EMPTY HOUSE?

An Empty House?

After rushing to the door Elizebeth starts knocking,

no answer...

She knocks on the window hoping that will prompt Jay to open the door,

no answer...

She returns to the door and knocks louder and harder. Eventually after all that knocking she tried the door and to her surprise it was already open. Worried and slightly confused she slowly opened the door and started looking around for any sign of Jay. After searching the living room Elizebeth started calling out "Jay?Jay? Where are you?Did you know your doors are open? Your curtains are still closed, are you still in bed?" Moving upstairs hoping to find Jay asleep in his room Elizebeth continues to call out until all the rooms had been searched.

No sign of him Elizebeth thought moving to the living room, *perhaps there was some paperwork that explained his whereabouts* she continued to think and upon searching Elizebeth started to uncover all of the old Whiskey bottles and glasses Jay had hidden all those days ago, fearing the worst Elizebeth bolted out of the house and started her search for Jay again hoping and praying that nothing bad was happening to Jay and that he was alright and in a sound state of mind.

THE BACK ALLEYS

The Back Alleys:

Elizabeth after searching all throughout Jay's house made her way to the town centre in Columbia hoping to have better luck locating his whereabouts, she began her search by first searching the open bars within the town knowing that Jay had been drinking it was the most logical first place to search or at least she thought so.

No luck…

With no real knowledge of the town of Columbia Elizebeth started asking the general public for information, person after person questioned and no new information was gained until finally she was finally given a small tidbit of information. A scruffy gentleman mentioned that she was only searching the "good" areas of the town and would most likely have a better chance of searching the other side of Columbia, the side considered to be "wrong side" of Columbia.

Hearing this Elizebeth continued her search checking alleyway after alleyway hoping that each she came across would have Jay there. A few hours passed and almost everywhere had been searched but just as she thought there was nowhere else she could do it, Elizabeth had found him. "Jay!" Elizabeth shouted rushing toward him, "I've been searching for you, I was so worried." But as she spoke her voice slowly dropped off, she was finally close enough to see Jay properly and finally able to see the disturbing, horrific state he was in.

ALIVE?

Alive?

A blood curdling horrific scene was set before Elizebeth, upon getting close to Jay she could see the vast amount of blood spouting from his neck and the deep wound that's causing it. Wasting no time Elizebeth, her hands trembling, calls for an ambulance making sure at the same point to keep pressure on his newly discovered wound trying her best to help keep him alive until the ambulance arrives.

Elizabeth, trying to keep Jay awake and alert, starts to speak with him.

"5 Minutes"

"The ambulance will be here in five minutes all I have to do is keep you alive and safe for five minutes."

"I'm sorry I took so long to find you"

"I should've stayed with you when I arrived no matter your answer"

"I love you and I will not let you die!"

Jay Swan, unable to speak clearly, starts to cry in Elizabeth's arms upon hearing her voice. He was overjoyed and crushingly sad she found him. Mixed emotions flood Jay's mind, happiness of his Love not being lost forever, Sadness of thinking he may still be unable to tell her how he truly feels, how he too loved her.

Sirens can be heard approaching and Elizebeth stands up to flag down the paramedics, before she leaves to get them Jay clutched to Elizabeth's arm and tries to speak to try and tell her one thing.

"I... I..."

Elizabeth shushed Jay telling him to save his strength and as she left to guide the paramedics, Jay just lay there in the alley and then before falling unconscious he heard a distant sound.

-Hisss

And then Darkness.

THE HOSPITAL

The Hospital:

"What is that bright light?"

Jay slowly opened his eyes, adjusting to the light and his surroundings as he did, the first thing he noticed was Elizabeth. Her head on his bed and her hand entwined with yours, he then realised where he was, a hospital. This revelation started bringing back memories bit by bit, remembering what had happened before he awoke in hospital, the nightmarish event that had transpired and how Elizebeth saved him and the words she spoke to him before he shut his eyes.

Jay looked over to Elizebeth who was still asleep next to him and as he did said with a weakened hoarse voice.

"I love you too Liz, thanks for coming back for me."

Tears started streaming down his face as he spoke, finishing his sentence he started wiping his eyes, drying his face from the tears. But then someone grabbed his hands, held them softly, Jay turned and saw Elizebeth, awake also with tears in her eyes smiling at him.

"You're okay! I'm so glad, I thought I had lost you."

Tears now streaming from the pair of them they sat and hugged each other for a long while ,crying and hugging, squeezing each other and muttering unintelligible words before eventually slowly moping up their tears and finally stopping, ending with them just smiling at each other pleased with each other's presence.

HONESTY

Honesty:

After a while Elizebeth broke the long silence with a single question.

"Did you mean that?"

Jay looked at her a little confused as to what she could mean, until finally he realised she had not been asleep after all, she had heard him say the words he wanted to say to her all along the words she longed to hear from him.

"Yes." Jay replied, smiling.

"I'm sorry I didn't mean what I said those few days ago."

"I have always loved you, since long ago and even now more than I ever thought possible"

Elizabeth looked at Jay with glee in her eye, *He finally said it, He finally said* it she thought, without a moment to lose she hugged Jay again, acknowledging what he had just said she whispered in his ear.

"I love you too."

THE BLACK CAT

The Black Cat:

After all had settled down both Elizebeth and Jay started talking about the few days they spent apart before the lifesaving reunion in the alleyway and then eventually what had led to Jay almost dying in that alleyway.

The conversation lasted hours with them both apologising for not being honest with one another and not being there to support one another as they had both wanted from the very start and eventually came the conversation of the alleyway and the black cat.

Jay spoke of the cat describing it as seemingly non threatening with its sleepy face and seeming dull claws. Its black fur and scarred skin. Its evil eyes and its ominous nature and aura.

Elizabeth keen to understand how Jay had been hurt listened intrigued and with full concentration never doubting his story and then when fully informed started thinking to herself in silence, skipping from thought to thought about this black cat and the nature of it. *Was it supernatural?" Was it simply feral?"*

Eventually she thanked Jay for speaking of this traumatic event consoling him and letting him know she will be there for him as she was for him before in his last traumatic situation all those years ago. Jay, overcome with happiness upon hearing this, hugged Elizebeth once more to thank her for understanding and being there for him.

A SMALL INVESTIGATION

A Small Investigation:

After a short talk with the doctors Elizebeth learned that Jay could return home soon, a few days at the most he would have to spend in the hospital. Knowing this she took up a new task whilst Jay recovers, a task to investigate that alleyway and the black cat Jay had described to her.

Elizebeth keen to uncover any information she could about the situation Jay found himself in and searched the alley for the black cat but to no avail, no sign of it, all that was left at the scene of the attack was Jay's dry blood on the cold concrete floor where he had been led bleeding out.

Elizebeth recounting that fateful day and the gruesome scene had to turn away from the view, heaving as she did trying as best she could to keep from throwing up. After a while she finished up her search taking only a few things with her as she left, a picture of the alleyway and what seemed to be fur or hair of some kind she found nearer the entrance of the alley.

Returning to the hospital Elizebeth sees that Jay is actually standing and is moving about in his room, rushing to his side after seeing this she congratulates him on the progress he's made on his recovery. Jay, happy to see her, invites Elizebeth to sit with him and speak of the future as they drink tea together as they had done over his recovery these last few days.

THE FUTURE

The Future:

The day had come for Jay to return home from the hospital and with Elizebeth at his side they left. The air was cool and the weather was nice and sunny. It has been almost a week since Jay has been outside and he took everything in as if it was the first time seeing it, smelling the air and looking around himself taking in the sights of the area. Elizabeth, noticing this, simply stared and smiled at him, allowing his moment of peace to last as long as he had wanted.

A short while later they had both arrived at Jay's house and at this point Elizebeth left his side at the door allowing Jay to enter on his own. Surprised Jay spun around and asked why she didn't follow him in. Elizabeth, confused by the question, didn't know what to say and simply stood there waiting for Jay to elaborate.

After a short pause Jay simply said, "Welcome Home!" Elizabeth then understood the question, she remembered they had discussed the future in the hospital and one topic was whether or not she would like to live with him. Not getting a straight answer at the hospital Jay was insisting on an answer to be made to stay.

Elizabeth simply nodded and entered the house content with the choice to stay with the one she loves. The one who also loves her back, remembering that Elizebeths face lit up with delight and glee knowing that their future together can only be one thing. Happy.

SOME TIME LATER

Some Time Later:

Day to day living returns to normal over time and both Jay and Elizebeth are happy and content with their life together with each other. Jay is able to continue his job as a psychiatrist virtually and Elizebeth happy to help him out with his work and happy to be out of the job she hated so long ago. Jay had stopped drinking so much to the advice of Elizebeth, his now significant other and Elizebeth, now more honest and less brash than before, helped him each step of the way.

AN UNSOLVED MYSTERY

An Unsolved Mystery:

Years go by and Jay and Elizabeth's relationship develops into a now normal stereotypical lifestyle, they had gotten married after spending time with each other and developing their relationship further as they had always wanted. Staying true to each other, honest and upfront helping their lives thrive together as time went on and loving each and every moment of their lives. Days pass and eventually a new adventure is discussed between Jay and Elizebeth, an adventure of fun and an adventure of investigation.

After all this time they could both still remember the black cat and that there was still no explanation about its origins or nature and as such a new place was found to investigate a place only known as "Rapture".

This investigation was meant to be simply lighthearted just to identify what the black cats nature was and get the answers they wanted but they also knew it could be incredibly dangerous and in knowing this took caution when they would eventually arrive at Rapture always planning ahead and sticking together at all times and above all else always listening for one key thing.

-Hisss

BLACK CAT TROIS: UNSOLVED MYSTERY

Quote: *"So I suppose you want to ask me what the Black Cat is"*

BIOS

Bios:

Jay Swan A 32-year-old Psychiatrist is traumatised by the loss of his left arm when he was Fourteen. Physically, he is built a bit like a scruffy blob. His top quality is that he is particularly straightforward and emotionally numb. He is striving to find acceptance of happiness and the regrets of his love life.

Elizabeth Songbird is A 31-year-old brash woman from the city who can only smile by day while working as a gardener. Physically, she is built like an elegant beautiful cat. She strongly dislikes her job and has been searching for her long lost friend and love interest.

RECAP

Recap:

Elizabeth searches for Jay after the rejection, The search entends to Jay's vacant house, The search goes to Columbia, Elizabeth finds injured Jay, Jay at Hospital, A Confession, Elizabeth Investigates the cat, Settled down and marriage, The start of a new adventure.

A NEW ADVENTURE

A New Adventure:

After some years a new adventure was discussed between Jay and Elizabeth, an adventure to uncover the unsolved mystery of the Black Cat. After all this time, after all these years they both still remember the Black Cat and that there was still no explanation of its nature or origins.

After some investigative digging together they came back to one bit of information: a city , a place known only as "Rapture". Days fly by as Jay and Elizabeth plan their trip of investigation, a trip meant to be somewhat nice and lighthearted simply to find out the Black Cat's nature and answer their burning questions they still had after all these years.

THE JOURNEY TO RAPTURE

The Journey To Rapture:

The time had come, Jay and Elizabeth were now fully prepared to set out on their journey to the city of Rapture. Leaving behind their new home and town of Columbia they both started their trip with a short car ride to the water's edge and their new transportation for the next few days, a boat.

Knowing little of the city they were journeying to, they spoke with one another during the long boat trip to set some rules of sorts for their arrival to this unknown, unfamiliar city. Knowing this trip could be incredibly dangerous they chose to ensure that they stick together no matter what to ensure the safety of one another.

The boat trip for the newlyweds was actually rather calm and enjoyable, with the sun and sea in view each day they took the opportunity to relax and spend time togetherwithout the stress to come from the investigation andunknown territory of the city of Rapture

THE BOAT

The Boat:

Almost a week passes on their boat trip and they know they must be getting close to this mysterious city when all of a sudden the captain stops the boat. Jay and Elizabeth look around confused as to why they stopped, they were in the middle of the sea, no land to be seen and nothing of note on the water.

After a short while Jay goes to the captain to ask why he has stopped the boat, "We're in the middle of nowhere, why are we stopping here? Is there a problem?" Jay asked quizzically. The captain answers with a simple remark, "We're here." Puzzled Jay takes another glance around the surrounding water of the boat to try and see what in the world the captain could mean by "Were here"

Suddenly the boat begins to rock to and fro, the water shifting and swirling. Elizabeth comes to join Jay to ask what's going on to catch up on any missed information. Then the captain comes beside them and points to the middle of the water off the side of the boat and says, "Watch closely now, this is quite the marvel to see." Jay and Elizabeth return their view to where the captain had pointed and there, in the middle nowhere, something began to rise out of the water.

With their mouths agape astonished at what they were witnessing, more and more of the structure began to break the surface of the water and become more and more apparent to what it could be. After some time the water settled… no more swirling and sloshing around, the boat was still.

The structure had fully surfaced and it was clear now what it was, Its rectangular shape and metallic structure was immediately identifiable.

It was an elevator…

The captain moved the boat closer to allow for boarding of the now visible elevator, and as Jay and Elizabeth did so he turned around and gave them a short wave as he sped off shouting one last phrase to the couple. "Good Luck, I'll return in a couple days when the elevator resurfaces, I hope you return safe and sound." And with that he was gone, slowly disappearing back into the distance, and then a familiar noise was heard.

-Ding

The elevator slowly closed and then began its descent...

THE UNDERWATER CITY

The Underwater City:

"An elevator? A bloody elevator!" Jay remarked,

"In the middle of nowhere, in the middle of the goddam sea!" Jay continued.

Elizabeth, still processing what was going on, simply nodded along with Jay's stammering about their current situation and circumstances. As the elevator kept descending deeper and deeper into the depths of the sea they both began to calm down and readjust to their current confusing conundrum of the event that just happened.

They began talking amongst themselves discussing where they were going believing that the only real answer that made sense must be Rapture City. A puzzling thing to encounter but not entirely unexpected when remembering its link to the Black Cat, their only link to the Black Cat.

After a while of decent they both heard that identifiable elevator ding again and now knew they were finally reaching the destination they were hoping for, the doors of the elevator slowly started to open and as they did both Elizabeth and Jay kept their eyes open to take in everything they could as quickly as they could to try and scope out danger if it were about, thankfully no threats were to be found yet and they both let out a sigh of relief stepping out of the elevator and finally entering the city of Rapture.

Rapture looked pretty unique in its appearance, there were houses, buildings and skyscrapers all under water, all connected with glass tube tunnel-like walkways reminiscent of an underwater aquarium. Looking out of the glass you could see transportation too, cars and bus like vehicles all propelling through the water to dock at each respective building or tube connections. The interior of each tube was pretty bare bones with only the framework of the structure visible with a red carpet lining each of the respective floors.

THE INVESTIGATION BEGINS

The Investigation Begins:

Following the tunnel set before them from the elevator, Jay and Elizabeth began their exploration and investigation of the area. Chatting among themselves about the scenery and how unbelievable it all seemed to be, they eventually found themselves in their first building within the city of Rapture.

"Beautiful" They said in sync.

The building interior looked like that of a royal hotel or expensive casino with red wallpaper and gold trimming around the skirting and ceiling respectively. The furniture looked pretty old but all seemed to fit the aesthetic of the building bringing out the feeling of a high class place. In the middle of the room stood what seemed to be a reception desk you'd find in hotel lobbies and upon seeing this the pair walked towards it in hopes to find someone to talk to.

Nobody in sight but there was a note stating if help was needed to ring the bell found on the counter, upon reading this and without wasting a single second they both collectively slapped that bell in unison. A short while passes but eventually somebody does come to the counter to the pair's surprise. "How can I help?" The new reception gentleman asked. A bit shocked and taken back, it took a while for Jay and Elizabeth to respond to the gentleman but eventually they began their questions.

They asked questions about the city of Rapture, how it came to be, how it was so secretive and mysterious, about the structures and transpiration of the city, the elevator and finally they asked about information regarding the Black Cat.

A CLUE

A Clue:

Answering their questions as best he could, the receptionist shed light upon each of their enquiries allowing them to better understand the city and what its nature is. After a while they came to the almighty question of the Black Cat. A bit taken back the receptionist was pretty shocked to hear of the question about the Black Cat and wondered how an outsider had encountered it. He explained that the Black Cat is a native animal exclusively residing in a remote part of the city of Rapture, and although it may look unthreatening it is without a shadow of a doubt a dangerous "being" he warned.

Following this new information new questions arose between everybody but the first to everybody's lips was how in the world this Black Cat came to be so far away from Rapture getting all the way to Columbia. Many theories were thought up but the most plausible is that someone from Rapture brought it to the land above water to wreak havoc on the uninformed unsuspecting public.

Eventually discussions circled back to the investigation at hand and the receptionist reluctantly told Elizabeth and Jay the location of the native area the Black Cats reside in. Warning the couple the receptionist said they shouldnt poke the bear as it were and leave it be as only danger can come about investigating further, unfortunately both Jay and Elizabeth said they had come too far to get answers and wanted them no matter the danger but they would be careful they assured the man.

After a brief rundown on the general area and directions to it shown on a crudely drawn map Jay and Elizabeth headed off towards their new investigation target, a place the receptionist called "The Depths".

THE DEPTHS

The Depths:

Following the provided instructions and map Jay and Elizabeth travelled towards the place known as "The Depths". Much like before they walked down the glass tunnel ways towards their goal destination taking in the gorgeous sea scenery as they went. Eventually they arrived at their objective, walking through a door marked with a wooden sign with the word "Depths" written on it in red. Slightly odd but they continued nonetheless.

The area was humid and dark, the pair was barely able to see what's ahead of them so they took the opportunity to stop and let their eyes adjust to the dim light level the area brought about. Walking slowly and carefully they stuck together knowing that this area was known as dangerous, keeping to their original plan for safety.

They searched and searched the area for what seemed like hours but in reality was only minutes, the darkness playing tricks with their mind and sense of time.

Eventually they made the decision to head back the way they came to readjust their minds to take a break from the stress and the darkness. Looking for the faint light they hoped to see as the doorway they suddenly heard movement around them.

Jay and Elizabeth froze in fear.

Not moving an inch they scanned ahead of them trying to see what was making the noise of movement they had heard but it was too dark to see much of anything let alone a potentially "Black Cat" they were both hoping and not hoping to find in the area called "The Depths".

A FAINT FAMILIAR SOUND

A Faint Familiar Sound:

Eventually the sound of movement seemed to fade away into the distance and when they thought it was safe Jay and Elizabeth turned and hugged one another, squeezing each other tight out of relief that the fear and potential threat was slowly going away. They stayed this way for a while before eventually taking up the task again to search for the doorway out of the depths.

Along the way new sounds started emerging every now and again, new sounds unknown to the couple, sounds that didn't seem threatening but were uneasy so they continued along their path towards what they hoped would be the direction of the exit.

As they continued further and further the sounds became a bit more familiar with each step they took, the sound of water, the sound of metal, the sound of carpeted flooring. And then the most memorable sound of all, the sound they dreaded to hear.

-Hisss

SPLIT UP

Split Up:

"RUN!"

They both yelled at each other sprinting off away from the direction of the sound hoping to distance themselves from it, further and further into the damp darkness they went praying to get away from that all too familiar noise. Thoughts spiralled in each of their heads…

"I'm going to die."

"Is it really the dreaded Black Cat?"

"Can we really escape?"

"Where's the exit?"

"I never should have come here."

"Please let us survive another day."

Eventually the noise was no longer able to be heard, slowing down their pace they began to come to a stop and finally take a breath after all that running. Leaning over with their hands on their knees taking huge gulps of air they looked around.

No…

No No No No NO!…

Jay couldn't see Elizabeth,

Elizabeth couldn't see Jay,

They'd lost each other in the frantic sprint. Lost each other in the darkness of The Depths.

A FATEFUL ENCOUNTER

A Fateful Encounter:

Cold, dark, wet and alone. Jay and Elizabeth had been separated in their escape of the suspected Black Cat. Looking around frantically in the hopes of seeing each other up close they both had a sinking feeling, they couldn't shout for each other in case the suspected Black Cat came toward their noise, they couldn't really move in any direction apart from forward in fears they may go towards the suspected Black Cat and with it the danger it would bring.

With no other choice the pair began walking forward away from the noise they heard in hopes it would somehow lead them back to each other again or at least to safety where they could then eventually regroup perhaps the doorway they had come from.

A few minutes pass and no sign of an exit or of each other.

Another handful of minutes passed and the darkness seemed to be endless, or so they thought, suddenly however a small speck of light was seen in front of them. Relief was felt by the pair and they hastily moved toward the light they assumed was the doorway they had entered from.

Unknown to the pair but Elizabrth was closer to the light than Jay was, the pair continued toward the light and eventually as the light grew closer and closer Elizabeth found the source of the light.

It was the receptionist with a flashlight.

Thankful she had someone to speak with and stick nearby to in the darkness Elizabeth let out a little sound squee of happiness.

Jay, following the light not too far behind Elizabeth's arrival heard the noise of excitement and rushed toward it knowing it was Elizabeth, eventually seeing her and the receptionist he rushed toward her hugging her tightly now knowing that she was thankfully safe and that the receptionist was their saviour in the darkness.

JUST IN TIME

Just In Time:

After arriving at the source of light now known as the receptionist they all took a short moment to regroup and figure out what to do next. They decided the smartest thing to do would be to leave The Depths and so they followed the receptionist talking with him as they went. "Why'd you come here? To save us?" They both asked him.

He told them he was worried about them after hearing they were investigating the Black Cat and actually headed toward The Depths after his warning earlier. He said he knew of the darkness of the area and thought it best he went to check on them to ensure that at the very least they would leave the area safe if they had gotten lost.

Approaching the doorway leaving The Depths theytold the receptionist how they had heard the -Hiss noise and that he helped them fully escape what they thought would be almost certain danger just in time.

Hearing them talk about this "-Hiss" the receptionist was pleased that he had taken it upon himself to help them out and within this thought he too heard the sound they described but from down the tunnel way not the darkness that was now behind them. Glancing down the direction of the noise he suddenly said.

"There! It's right there! I see it!"

Jay and Elizabeth both follow the gaze of the receptionist to see the source of the noise and sure enough sat at the end of the tunnel way was the Black Cat.

THE CHASE

The Chase:

Without skipping a beat both Jay and Elizabeth took off toward the Black Cat to give chase, they thought that capturing the Black Cat or interacting with it in some way might yield the answers of its emergence. They felt that following the Black Cat may lead to something bigger and more informative, something more concrete about its creation and mystery.

They chased it in and out of numerous buildings and countless tunnels eventually following it to a new set of stairs leading upward towards the surface they hadn't seen in some time. Keeping on the Black Cats trail they followed it up and up and up and up until finally they reached the top of the stairs where there was a single door leading outside.

Pushing forward out of the door they came to realise they were now on an isolated island with a single structure built upon it.

A Lighthouse.

THE LIGHTHOUSE

The Lighthouse:

Now on the surface they could see standing before them was a towering red and white striped lighthouse and the Black Cat they were chasing was now nowhere to be seen. With a quick look around and no Black Cat in sight the only thing that made sense in the moment was to investigate the newly found lighthouse.

Jay and Elizabeth approached the lighthouse keeping an eye out for the Black Cat they had been following and eventually came up to the door. The door seemed relatively old and weathered with no visible lock to be seen, knowing this Elizabeth tried the handle and with a loud creak the door sluggishly opened before them revealing a spiralling staircase up to the top of the lighthouse where the beam and controls were kept.

Pushing their way inside the couple started their journey up their next flight of stairs with each step they took leaving an audible echo all the way around the tower. After some time they eventually made it to the top of the lighthouse and began looking around to search for anything of use of value, eventually coming to the light controls.

Jay nonchalantly tried the big switch expecting nothing to happen since it was so old and decrepit looking when all of a sudden a blindly bright light came beaming out of the mechanism in front of them. Flabbergasted by the light actually working they had a look around at the scenery that was now illuminated, the only thing visible by the light was a single island shack connected by a small bridge to the lighthouse island.

Jay and Elizabeth looked at each other slightly confused that the light isn't spinning or changing direction as they knew lighthouses to do and then it dawned on them, perhaps it's not broken it's simply showing us what we want to see. Upon realising this revelation they made their way back down the lighthouse now knowing their new destination is the newly illuminated shack nearby.

ORIGINS

Origins:

Reaching the bottom of the lighthouse and setting foot on the isolated island once more Jay and Elizabeth looked toward the direction of the light and made their way toward the connecting bridge in the same direction. The bridge was hardly visible being just at the water's surface and made of the same glass as Rapture, but nevertheless they proceeded gingerly across the bridge to the newly illuminated shack.

Upon arriving at the shack they started to hear what seemed to be purring and the pita patter of little paws, keeping together they slowly opened the shack door to see what was within its walls and to their surprise it was the Black Cat but it seemed a lot more docile than before, like it was accustomed to their presence now or simply didn't care about their arrival and intrusion into its home.

Entering the shack and being weary of the Black Cat still Jay and Elizabeth began to rummage through the shacks interior looking though whatever they could find and read. Eventually Elizabeth came across some strewn papers that had diagrams of the Black Cat and small handwritten notes alongside. Seeing this she ushered Jay to the documents she had found and the pair of them began to read the information presented before them.

Pages and pages of information about the Black Cat were scattered all across this shack and all contained diagrams of the Black Cat not sketches or drawings but diagrams. This led the pair to believe that the Black Cat was in fact manufactured and not actually a living being, or maybe a living Chimaera of sorts and after a while of more searching their beliefs were well justified.

The pair came across a single leaflet, a leaflet advertising the Black Cat Chimaeras.

The leaflet showed little tidbits of information, mainly advertising the fact that you could get a well trained pet or guard animal for your home namely the chimaera in question, the Black Cat. Alongside the leaflet was a small historical background on what the chimaera was exactly to better explain it origins, and it states that they were brought about from the idea around the greek mythology chimaera and how the image was adapted to be more pleasing in a way to a consumer as a modge podge animal would be more scary than not as a pet.

Jay and Elizabeth looked at each other after reading this and let out a small relieved sigh, they thought at least it wasn't a demon or something super evil after all this time. It was simply an experimental pet guard pet thing that was exclusively distributed around Rapture. A few more moments went by and the pair continued to read the available information in the shack before eventually deciding it was time to go. They made their way to the door with a single returning glance at the Black Cat still in the shack bidding farewell to it after they left.

MYSTERY SOLVED

Mystery Solved:

After Jay and Elizabeth left the shack they came together to compile the information they had just garnered from the shack and started recording all their findings in a single black journal, being happy the investigation is finally at an end and the mystery is finally solved.

It was still pretty light out on the island and from a distance they could see the boat they had taken to the elevator, elated to see the captain again both Jay and Elizabeth began waving their arms and calling out to him in hopes to catch his attention and be able to once again board his boat and leave to return home.

Thankfully the captain saw the couple and approached the island they were at, signalling them to make their way aboard once he was close enough.

After clambering onto the boat they asked the captain to return them home as their trip to Rapture was over, being the kind man he was he agreed and they set off on their return journey home.

RETURNING HOME

Returning Home:

The journey home took almost a week as it did for their arrival but this time it seemed to fly by, Jay and Elizabeth shared the story of their trip to Rapture and the truth behind the Black Cat they were investigating with the captain and the captain shared his thoughts about it too including his own story on his own interaction with the elevator and the sea life that inhabited the waters near it.

Their conversations seemed to last so little time but to their surprise they arrived at the dock near their home in what seemed like such a short time even though it was almost a week. Bidding farewell to the captain Jay and Elizabeth deboarded the ship and set off toward home.

During the car trip Jay brought up the attack he had been through with the Black Cat in the past and surmised that it must've been protecting its owner of Rapture in that same alley he entered that fateful day.

Now knowing they were sold and used as guard pets made a small bit more sense on how it got out of Rapture and why it attacked in the first place. Leaving this as his hopeful explanation of that day he felt he may be able to get over his traumatic experience with time knowing it wasn't just some freak event.

LIFE WITH THE ANSWERS

Life With The Answers:

After Jay and Elizabeth arrived home they compiled their notes and the black journal they had recorded their findings on and decided they wanted to make this information known to the public in any way they could, whether people believed the story or not did not matter as long as the findings and their adventure was known to the public.

And so they wrote a series of books about their lives before their encounter with the car and about their adventure regarding this Black Cat, the mystery of the Black Cat, the danger of the Black Cat and of course the conclusion of their investigation of the Black Cat Chimaera. This series of books would simply been known under the title "Black Cat"

THE END

The End:

The book series was a smashing success and with it Jay and Elizabeth came to know fame and a small fortune, they continued their lives as they did before their adventure living happily together now with a clear mindset and no burning unresolved questions.

Eventually they came to have two kids of their own which they told their stories to and brought up as best they could, providing them with all they could ever need with their wealth they amassed from their book sales, leading them to be brought up well and self sufficient before they both came to have their eventual death together of old age in ever loving happiness together knowing their kids will always be okay and they will always love one another,

ABOUT THE AUTHOR

About The Author:

I like to think I'm just a regular person with the odd scrambled idea and nothing else.

BOOKS BY THE AUTHOR

Books By The Author:

Black Cat - The first in the series of the Black Cat books.

Black Cat Deux - The second instalment of the Black Cat book series.

Black Car Trois - The final instalment of the Black Car book series.